Jean M. Akam, the daughter of a librarian, was introduced to books at an early age. Able to read by five years of age, this opened up a visual world of adventure, fantasy and fun.

She has written short stories for adults, had poetry published, plus a story in an anthology about Colchester, where she lives. This is her first children's book and she would like to expand her readers' imaginations.

THE VIRTUAL REALITY SPACE PIRATES

(A FUTURISTIC SHORT STORY OF SPACE PIRATES AND YOUNG HEROES)

Jean M. Akam

THE VIRTUAL REALITY SPACE PIRATES

(A FUTURISTIC SHORT STORY OF SPACE PIRATES AND YOUNG HEROES)

Nightingale Books

NIGHTINGALE PAPERBACK

A CIP catalogue record for this title is
available from the British Library.

ISBN 978 1 907552 78 6

*Nightingale Books is an imprint of
Pegasus Elliot MacKenzie Publishers Ltd.*
www.pegasuspublishers.com

First Published in 2016

**Nightingale Books
Sheraton House Castle Park
Cambridge England**

Printed & Bound in Great Britain

To my grandchildren, Gemma, Jake and Molly.
Also Rory Dunbar, who was the first young person
to read the story.

Acknowledgements

I would like to thank Rory Dunbar for his helpful comments. Also to the staff at Pegasus who have been so helpful, bringing my first children's book to life.

Chapter 1

The Adventure Begins

Veryan was starting to get annoyed. As if it wasn't enough that the Space Pirate, Gadran, whom he had been chasing across the Galaxy, had gone to ground on his home planet, Plutora, Veryan's assistant, Nayma, had told him they had four intruders on deck 3b. Veryan's ship, the VSS Terra Mina, had been static above Plutora since Gadran, whom they had been chasing in his pirate ship, the Garda Luca, had docked in a space bay on that planet.

No sign of life could be seen on Plutora's surface. Veryan could only watch as Gadran made it through the shield gate in the Planet's defence system, which had closed leaving Veryan outside. The only way it could be opened was by equipment to be found on Plutoran pirate vessels. He watched Gadran docking on the Planet on his space screen.

The boomerang shaped ship, with its upper deck shaped like a skull, had docked in a similarly shaped hole in Plutora's surface. Its inhabitants were mostly space pirates who lived in a number of underground tunnels when they weren't plundering and looting in space.

The only thing visible on the Planet's surface were 1000's of skull-like shapes. These were the cockpits of the Plutoran pirate fleet. They were black and the holes in them which looked like eye sockets were the vessel's viewing ports. The hole for the nose was where the banks of Plutoran cannons shot at their victim's ships and the mouth was the docking bay for their marauding, mini attack vessels. Their appearance was sinister and designed to put people off attacking the Plutorans. The planet was also constructed in Micronium, a metal that was difficult to penetrate with weapon fire.

Veryan fumed. It was his first command and everything was going wrong. His ship was supposed to be faster than Gadran's, but they had hit a meteor storm and Gadran had used the cover it offered to escape. Time was of the essence. If Veryan didn't get the crystal back that Gadran had stolen from Veryan's Planet, Varga, the Vargans would be at war again with Malparnia. He couldn't even bear to think about it – about the fact his marriage to Alva, the President of Malparnia, Colmar's Daughter, would be off and their planets would return to the warring that had been going on between them for centuries. It had started with a feud whose beginning no one could even remember.

Veryan's face softened as he thought of Alva. They had met at the International Space Academy on Qtari 4. When he met her he hadn't realised she belonged to the enemy as all students at the Academy were not allowed to tell anyone where they had come from. This was sometimes difficult as many of the students gave away their roots by their appearance. After all, where else in space, out in the virtual reality suite. Veryan in those days had been a bit arrogant. He was so sure of himself and his prowess at space jousting. No one on Varga had ever beaten him. When he was knocked off his virtual horse by his unknown opponent he was amazed, but thought it just a freak happening. Perhaps he had not put his virtual reality equipment on correctly – he had put it on rather fast as he had overslept and had been a bit late. He wasn't yet used to the discipline at the Academy. As he was the President of Varga's Son, at home he had got away with many things he couldn't get away with at the Academy. His Father, Druizz, worried about his Son's behaviour, had sent him to the Academy to be brought down a peg or two. When his opponent had taken the equipment off, Veryan had been shattered to find that his opponent was a girl. "Oh the shame of it," thought Veryan. How could he ever face anyone again.

However, the girl just shook him by the hand, smiled at him and wandered off. Veryan was immediately taken with her smile – it lit up her whole face. However, when he came to his senses he had visions of her in the food bar boasting about how she had beaten him. This fear he found to be quite unfounded and his defeat was never mentioned. He began to search her out as he found that she had

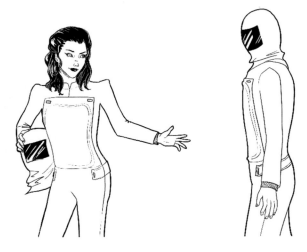

total confidence in her abilities and never boasted whenever she achieved some feat or other. After a while they became viewed as boyfriend and girlfriend and people left them alone. There was a certain excitement in their relationship as it had to be kept secret from the Director of the Academy who would have banned it.

It was only later that Veryan found out who she was. He had gone to call for her to go to classes and had walked into her room to find her on the space screen interactor to her Father. Veryan was stunned. What was Alva doing talking to his Planet's enemy. He left the room quickly.

Later, Alva found him brooding, "Why did you leave my room so fast?" she asked.

"What are you doing talking to Colmar, my Planet's worst enemy ?" asked Veryan. Alva turned white.

"He's my Father," she said. Veryan was speechless. He cursed the Academy for its policy of people having to be anonymous. If he had known who Alva was in the beginning he wouldn't have touched her with a barge pole. As everyone at the Academy had to speak Spatial Esperanto so there was a common language and Alva looked like a girl from his Planet it had never crossed his mind she came from the enemy planet.

"Come and talk," said Alva, "if we can get on so well together, if our planets forgot the feud for a while, who knows perhaps we could make peace and all live in harmony."

They had eventually talked to their fathers, who after the initial shock discussed the idea with their councils. If the truth were known they were both sick of all the fighting. It had become very costly and they had lost quite a few good friends during it. Colmar and Druizz, convened for talks on the neutral Planet, Lugari 9, with the council of that planet acting as go-betweens and decided to give it a try. It was agreed, as a gesture of goodwill, in order to cement

this new alliance their children would be allowed to get married.

To honour the agreement they exchanged rare crystals, the only two like it in the Universe. Druizz, gave the crystal for safe keeping into the hands of his trusted advisor, a man called Gadran. Later, he was to discover handing over the crystal to this man was a big mistake. He had trusted Gadran totally. Gadran had always offered him good advice and had appeared very honest. Too late, Druizz discovered that Gadran was a spy from the Planet, Plutora. He discovered this when they had returned from the meeting with the Malparnians. No one had seen Gadran since the council meeting. They had seen him pick up the crystal and had heard him say that he was taking it back to the ship. After a few hours a message was received from Gadran, that if Druizz did not send him a large amount of Vargan space dubloons within seventy-two space hours then he would let Colmar know how careless they had been with his crystal. It would have been seen as an insult by Colmar and all the Malparnians and war would have been declared again. So Veryan had been despatched on the 'Terra Mina' to hunt Gadran down. His Sister, Jazza and Brother, Rannal, had volunteered to go with him.

Chapter 3

The Intruders

Veryan was alerted to the intruders again by Nayma. She asked him if he wanted to send two droids down to deck 3B to find out who was down there. Jazza and Rannal also volunteered to go and left the flight deck with Zoid and Zenoid, their own personal, guard Droids. The Droids had been invented after the war with Malparnia had been depleting the Planet of its young people. They were virtually indestructible, therefore very cost effective.

On deck 3B were Gemma, Rory, Molly and Jake and they should not have been there. They were schoolchildren from Earth in the year 2150 A.D. Their class had been on a visit to the Museum of Virtual Reality with their teacher, Mr. Mason. He had told them all to stay together when they arrived but after playing a few games in the Museum, Molly had found a door which said 'Private, No Entry to the

Public'. As they were all a bit bored they dared each other to go through the door.

All they found after Rory had bravely stuck his head round the door was a table with some virtual reality head sets on it next to a large computer like machine with touch screen instructions and nothing else. All the walls were bare. "I wonder what all the fuss is about?" said Jake.

"Why don't we try the head sets?" asked Molly.

"I don't think we should, there must be some reason nobody is allowed in here", Rory answered her.

"I dare you to put the head set on" said Molly. Rory could never resist a dare and so he put it on. Molly uttered a small giggle and pressed her finger on an onscreen text box which stated 'Adventures in Space'.

"What can you see?", they all shouted.

"I think I'm on a space ship. I can see a long metal corridor with windows and outside it is all black with occasional stars and planets", said Rory excitedly.

"Why don't you all put the head sets on, it seems quite safe. There is no one around." They did as he suggested and joined Joss on what turned out to be deck 3B. They were the intruders.

The children gazed out of the viewing ports in wonder. They were so busy looking out of these that they did not hear the approach of the Droids until it was too late. The Droids drew their space weapons and pointed them at the children. Rory heard a noise and turned around to see two three metre high Droids.

They were a shiny, metallic purple and were constructed out of rings and strips of metal with a red visor where their vision system was. Rory yelled at the others to get their masks off so they could get out of the virtual space ship and the danger it seemed to present to the four of them. They all tugged at the masks, but to their horror found that they could not remove them. Next thing they felt was a funny feeling in their heads and they all fell over unable to move. Zoid and Zenoid had used their weapons' stun power. The children were then picked up bodily by the Droids, one child in each metal arm and taken up to the flight deck, accompanied by a surprised Rannal and Jazza. "They're only Earth children," Rannal told Veryan. Veryan was not so sure, some of the planets had

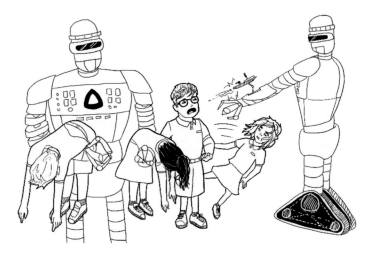

very small but vicious inhabitants and he eyed the children warily. He asked them what they were doing on his ship and they told him how they had disobeyed the rules at the Museum and had landed on Veryan's space ship by mistake. Veryan was angry. He had enough to do without having to work out how to get the four of them back to Earth and to the year 2150 they had left.

"I'm sorry but I can't get you back to Earth yet," he said to them," Jazza will explain what is going on to you." As he was talking to them the face of a pirate appeared on Veryan's space screen. The

children gazed at him in amazement. He looked just like the pirates that they had seen in old films, with long, black hair, black pointed teeth and a black patch around his left eye. There was also a large skull shaped earring in his left ear lobe.

"Who are you," Veryan asked the on screen image.

"Don't you recognise me?" the image asked Veryan.

"Your voice sounds familiar, said Veryan, but I am finding it hard to place you as I don't mix with pirates. I say pirates as you are transmitting from a pirate planet and you are dressed like one."

The image uttered a deep, rumbling laugh and then smirked at Veryan and said "I am Gadran your Father's trusted advisor." Veryan and his crew stared in disbelief as Gadran's appearance had totally changed from when he was Druizz's advisor. He now looked sinister. "Have you got the ransom money?" he asked Veryan.

"I'll see you in Largal first, before I give you any money." answered Veryan.

"What's Largal?" Rory wanted to know.

"It's a black hole where Plutoran prisoners are sent until someone pays their ransom," said Rannal.

"We'll see about that," said Gadran as he disappeared from the screen.

There was a humming sound and all of a sudden a bright light surrounded Veryan and Nayma. They then disappeared. Rannal and Jazza took command and ordered the Droids to scan the *Terra Mina* for signs of Veryan and his assistant. Whilst this was going on they filled in Rory and his friends on what had been happening. The four offered to help in any way they could as they felt a bit guilty about Veryan's disappearance. Whilst he was involved in discovering who they were he had lowered the internal defence shields on the ship in order to find them and had left himself wide open to what had happened. Gadran then appeared on the screen again and told Rannal that Veryan had got his way and was now in Largal and the ransom money had increased. If he did not get the money, four million Vargan Space dubloons within the next twenty-four hours they would never see Veryan, Nayma or the crystal again.

They all looked gloomy. Rannal and Jazza were about the same age as the children but had been taught how to fly the space ship from an early age. Their brains were a lot larger than Earth children's brains and therefore they were able to cope with adult type problems. They all had a brain storming session – it was a big problem. No one had ever come out of Largal unless a ransom had been paid. Rannal knew that Varga did not have the sort of money that Gadran was demanding. Even though he had been taught to fly the ship, Largal had a defence shield and if he was lucky enough to get through the shield he would then be confronted with the Karn Vortex. This was made up of whirling black light that affected brain patterns unless you had the right protective shield equipment. Many people were now Plutoran slaves as they had not taken the right precautions before entering the Vortex or their planets had not had enough money to ransom them.

Rannal and Jazza could not bear to think of Veryan and Nayma suffering this sort of fate. Even though they all thought long and hard no one could think of a solution. Time was running out. All of a sudden Zenoid spoke in his tinny type voice. "How about using Krell Drive?" he suggested. Jazza looked worried.

"Is this the only solution we have," she said? No one had used Krell Drive for centuries and she had forgotten where the equipment was.

"Follow me," said Zoid, it is risky but I think it is the only solution we have left." They followed him to deck 14C and he pressed a small, metal square on the wall. Two doors slid open and inside they all saw a large glowing circle with a machine with a bank of buttons in front of it.

"What on earth is this?" said Gemma. She was the quietest of the children but she had started to feel worried. The children learned that Krell Drive had once been used by the Vargans to go backwards in time so they knew what their enemies would do before it happened and so could defeat them. However, it had started to malfunction and had not been used since its inventor and most of the scientists on Varga had one day disappeared without trace. It had then been considered dangerous and had not been touched for years. However, it was their only option. Rannal hurriedly programmed Zenoid for the information on how to use the equipment.

"Wait a moment," said Jake. "if we are all meant to go back in time what will happen to us?"

"You will find yourself back at the Museum," said Jazza.

"We will go back to before the crystal was stolen and be able to stop it happening as we know all about Gadran's intentions now."

"We would love to see you again," said Molly to Jazza.

"You will," Jazza answered. "When you get to the Museum look at the virtual reality games menu for the program marked 'Vargan Adventures'.

"Hurry, we have to go." They all stood on the glowing circle in the centre of the room. Zoid's arm extended to the bank of buttons and he pressed two – one to send the children back to the year 2150 on Earth and the other to send the rest of them back to Lugari 9, prior to the crystal being handed over.

Chapter 4

The Conclusion – Watch This Space

The children found themselves in the entrance to the Museum. No one seemed to have noticed anything; in fact the school party hadn't started to go round the Museum yet. The children, when the enormity of what they had just experienced had sunk in, went to find the door they had gone through before, the door marked, 'Private. No admittance to the Public.' "Let's go and look at the virtual reality menu," said Rory. They entered the room and looked at the instructions. When they came to the one called 'The Virtual Reality Space Pirates' a message flashed up' Put on Space Visors to continue'. They all did as instructed and found themselves outside a large, white building. It had a sign outside that said 'Vargan Marriage Centre'.

They walked up the steps and through a blue, metallic door which slid open silently as they walked towards it. On entering the room which had a huge glass-like ceiling they noticed that in the middle of it were Veryan and a very pretty girl. Standing near them were Jazza and Rannal and two men. Veryan and the girl were holding a crystal each and they exchanged them in turn; when this happened the two men shook hands and walked towards the door smiling.

Jazza suddenly noticed Joss and the others and walked over. "Is that Alva?" Said Gemma.

"Yes," said Jazza. She informed the children that Gadran had been arrested after he had confessed to a plot to steal the crystal. Everyone was pleased that everything had turned out right.

"Can we see you again," said Molly to Jazza.

"Of course, you can," Jazza answered. "Just visit the Museum. In virtual reality we can always be here. Whenever you get bored come and see us and we can share more adventures."

The four took their visors off and they were back in the Museum – back to a different sort of reality unable to tell anyone of their adventures as none of them fancied being in detention for disobeying the sign 'Not open to the public' on the Virtual Reality Room door. However, they all made a pact that they would return as soon as they could to their new friends in their virtual reality world.